First published in 2016 by Nosy Crow Ltd
The Crow's Nest, 10a Lant Street
London SE1 1QR
www.nosycrow.com

This edition published in 2016

ISBN 978 0 85763 407 8 (PB)

Nosy Crow and associated logos are trademarks
and/or registered trademarks of Nosy Crow Ltd.

Text copyright © Jane Clarke 2016
Illustrations copyright © Migy Blanco 2016

The right of Jane Clarke to be identified as the author of this work
and of Migy Blanco to be identified as the illustrator of this work has been asserted.

A CIP catalogue record for this book is available from the British Library.

Printed in China
Papers used by Nosy Crow are made from
wood grown in sustainable forests.

10 9 8 7 6 5 4 3 2 1 (PB)

To Sammy,
with love from Grandma
J.C.

For Meki with love
M.B.

OLD MACDONALD'S
things that
GO

Jane Clarke

Illustrated
by
Migy Blanco

nosy crow

Old Macdonald had a farm.
He loved things that go!

And on that farm
he had a bike.
He loved things that go!

With a ding-a-ling here,
and a ding-a-ling there.
Here a ding, there a ling,
everywhere a ding-a-ling.

Old Macdonald had a farm.
He loved things that go!

And on that farm
he had a car.
He loved things that go!

With a vroom-vroom here,
and a vroom-vroom there.
Here a vroom, there a vroom,
everywhere a vroom-vroom.

Old Macdonald had a farm.
He loved things that go!

And on that farm
he had a tractor.
He loved things that go!

With a chugga-chugga here,
and a chugga-chugga there.
Here a chugga, there a chugga,
everywhere a chugga-chugga.

Old Macdonald had a farm.
He loved things that go!

And on that farm
he had a combine harvester.
He loved things that go!

With a rattle-swish here,
and a rattle-swish there.
Here a rattle, there a swish,
everywhere a rattle-swish.

Old Macdonald had a farm.
He loved things that go!

And on that farm
he had a bus.
He loved things that go!

With a beep-beep here,
and a beep-beep there.
Here a beep, there a beep,
everywhere a beep-beep.

Old Macdonald had a farm.
He loved things that go!

And on that farm
he had a boat.
He loved things that go!

With a swoosh-swoosh here,
and a swoosh-swoosh there.
Here a swoosh, there a swoosh,
everywhere a swoosh-swoosh.

Old Macdonald had a farm.
He loved things that go!

And on that farm
he had a digger.
He loved things that go!

With a dig-dig here,
and a dig-dig there.
Here a dig, there a dig,
everywhere a dig-dig.

Old Macdonald had a farm.
He loved things that go!

And on that farm
he had a fire truck.
He loved things that go!

With a nee-naw here,
and a nee-naw there.
Here a nee, there a naw,
everywhere a nee-naw.

Old Macdonald had a farm.
He loved things that go!

And on that farm
he had a train.
He loved things that go!

With a choo-choo here,
and a choo-choo there.
Here a choo, there a choo,
everywhere a choo-choo.

Old Macdonald had a farm.
He loved things that go!

And on that farm he had a plane.
He loved things that go!

With a zoom-zoom here,
and a zoom-zoom there.
Here a zoom, there a zoom,
everywhere a zoom-zoom.

Old Macdonald had a farm.
He loved things that go . . .

With a choo-choo here,
and a choo-choo there.
Here a choo, there a choo,
everywhere a choo-choo.

Nee-naw here,
nee-naw there.
Here a nee, there a naw,
everywhere a nee-naw.

Dig-dig here,
dig-dig there.
Here a dig, there a dig,
everywhere a dig-dig.

Swoosh-swoosh here,
swoosh-swoosh there.
Here a swoosh, there a swoosh,
everywhere a swoosh-swoosh.

Beep-beep here,
beep-beep there.
Here a beep, there a beep,
everywhere a beep-beep.

Rattle-swish here,
rattle-swish there.
Here a rattle, there a swish,
everywhere a rattle-swish.

Chugga-chugga here,
chugga-chugga there.
Here a chugga, there a chugga,
everywhere a chugga-chugga.

Vroom-vroom here,
vroom-vroom there.
Here a vroom, there a vroom,
everywhere a vroom-vroom.

Ding-a-ling here,
ding-a-ling there.
Here a ding, there a ling,
everywhere a ding-a-ling.

Old Macdonald had a farm . . .

...He loved things that go!